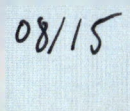

The Spirit of Love

By Caroline Keefer
and Sandra Brown

AuthorHouse™ LLC
1663 Liberty Drive
Bloomington, IN 47403
www.authorhouse.com
Phone: 1-800-839-8640

© 2013 Sandra Brown and Caroline Keefer. All rights reserved.

No part of this book may be reproduced, stored in a retrieval system, or transmitted by any means without the written permission of the author.

Published by AuthorHouse 08/10/2013

ISBN: 978-1-4918-0652-4 (sc)
ISBN: 978-1-4918-0653-1 (e)

Library of Congress Control Number: 2013914049

Any people depicted in stock imagery provided by Thinkstock are models, and such images are being used for illustrative purposes only.
Certain stock imagery © Thinkstock.

This book is printed on acid-free paper.

Because of the dynamic nature of the Internet, any web addresses or links contained in this book may have changed since publication and may no longer be valid. The views expressed in this work are solely those of the author and do not necessarily reflect the views of the publisher, and the publisher hereby disclaims any responsibility for them.

The Spirit of Love

By Caroline Keefer and Sandra Brown

PENDER COUNTY PUBLIC LIBRARY
BURGAW, NORTH CAROLINA

Once upon a time at the very top of planet earth, a potentially tragic yet ultimately magical journey began. The temperature was 30 degrees below zero, the ice beneath the drifts of snow was a mile thick, and the 50 mile per hour wind hurled pellets of ice that stung like arrows. Visibility was less than the length of a soccer field.

The isolated tundra seemed endless. One thing for sure, no one or nothing could possibly survive there except some well-prepared scientists who were on a mission of mercy.

This team of dedicated scientists was hundreds of miles away and included explorers and medical personnel. They were getting ready to begin their daily missions. The Polar Bear Rescue and Rehabilitation Center was established in January 2012. It had been a struggle. Years of planning, hard work and fund raising had paved the way to the opening of the center.

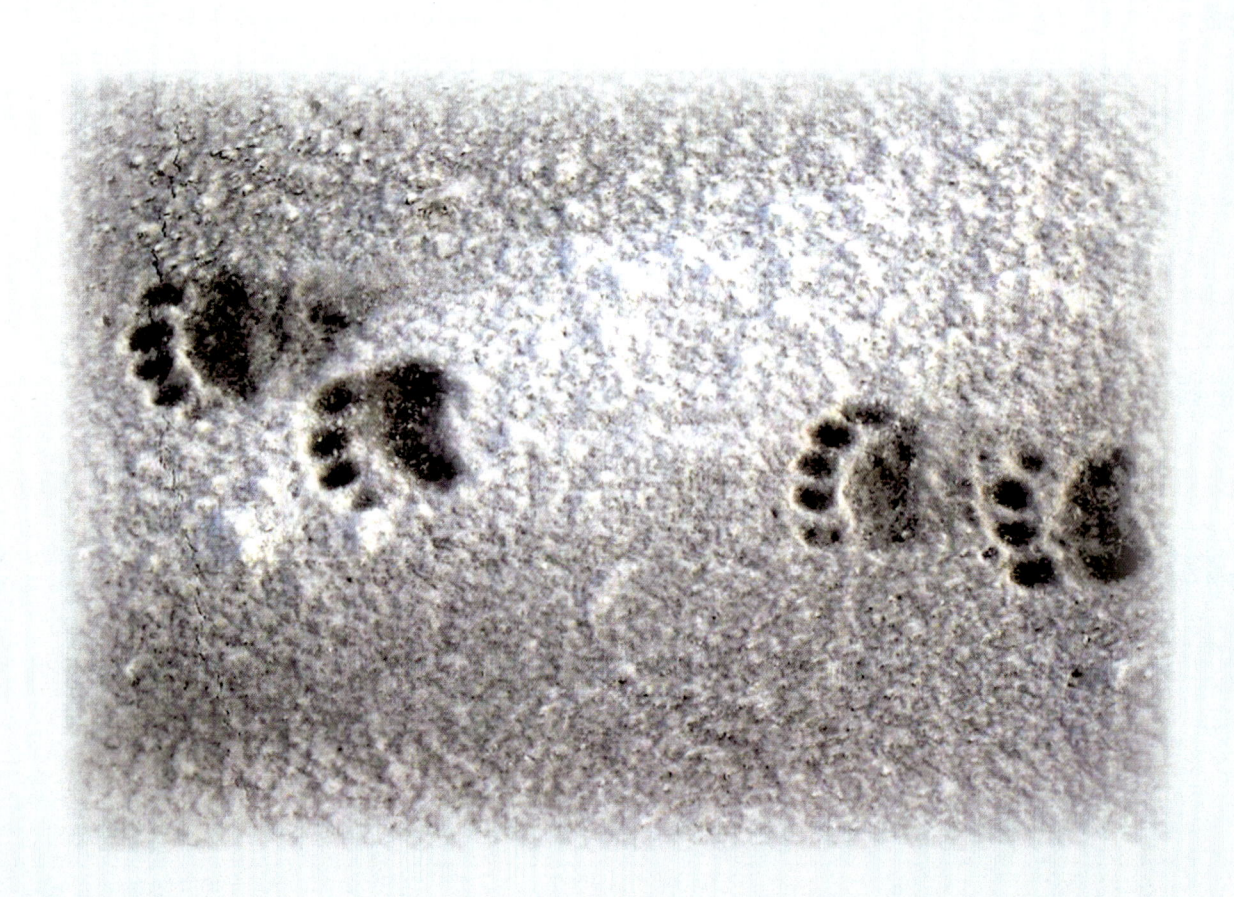

The Arctic is the only place in the world where polar bears live and the evidence suggested that the population was declining. Rescue was needed.

Today's missions would include observation of polar bear behavior and looking for any signs of sick or abandoned bears. The ventures would include exploring areas around the sea ice. Their searches rarely focused inland. Dog sleds and sea planes were used as their primary search transportation. Helicopter pilots would be on alert if any rescue was needed.

As their separate treks began, everything seemed to be normal. In fact these missions seemed to be so routine two pilots spontaneously decided to venture further inland, deeper into the wilderness than usual. Fuel was running low and the seaplane was about to turn back to the base.

Suddenly, the co-pilot thought he saw something move in the snow. He told the pilot to turn around. The pilot laughed and said, "Impossible, nothing would be this far out. All of our sightings have been closer to the polar bear's favorite food, seals." But the co-pilot was insistent upon seeing something so they circled the spot where the co-pilot saw the movement one more time. It was late. The blue sky was quickly disappearing. But in the sliver of light remaining the two pilots agreed that there was something alive on top of the snow.

"We must radio the base and see if a helicopter can be dispatched immediately." Using a GPS they gave the helicopter pilots the exact location of their sighting. The crews back at the base were incredulous. Yet, this was their business and they could not take a chance of losing a bear. They took off.

Time was short. The weather radar showed a storm moving in on their destination. A blizzard to contend with was all the more reason to hurry. If the seaplane's pilots had seen a bear, the storm might be the end of it..

They reached the spot where the seaplane's plots had marked on the GPS.

As they hovered over the sighting this is what they saw!

A tiny animal appeared. Nothing to eat, not another polar bear within miles. This was an impossibility.

They quickly radioed headquarters. They also contacted pilots of the search plane that was now circling above. "Congratulations! There is life below.!" Again they saw movement. The cub was running. He was frightened by the noise and the tremendous wind created by the helicopter. Both pilots hit the ground running toward where they thought the bear would be.

A pair of huge brown eyes appeared from a drift of snow. The cub looked thin and appeared weak, but his eyes showed it all. He was glad to see them. He had hope and it shown in his eyes.

The wind was howling and the helicopter pilots contacted the base. "We have picked up a polar bear cub." The message from headquarters was brief—"bring him to the rescue center immediately!"

The cub seemed to understand. He quietly settled into the warm blanket that the co-pilot wrapped around him and went to sleep. He was exhausted.

When the rescue crew reached the rescue and rehab center the mood was one of cautious celebration. The cub was alive, but would he survive? Unanswered questions were the source of their conversations.

"A polar bear cub cannot survive in the wild without his mother. How did the bear get so far into the wilderness?

Where was his family? Will he live? If he does live what will happen to him?"

As the minutes turned into hours and the hours into days, one question was answered. THE CUB WOULD SURVIVE!

Another phase of the operation began, find the cubs family. They dispatched helicopters into the snow to search for a trace of the cub's origins. Most of all they hoped to find his mother. Using the spot where he was found at the beginning point, the seaplane flew increasingly large circles as they searched. As hours passed, hopes grew dim that the cub's relatives would be found. The only good news was that the family was most likely alive, but they must have moved on to another hunting site.

After two long days of searching the explorers began to focus on possible other polar bear families that may adopt the baby bear. The task was difficult. All the the families they focused on seemed to be intact and the cubs that were with them were older. They doubted the mothers in those families would adopt a young and needy cub.

The caregivers marveled at how quickly the baby bear was regaining his strength. They were equally surprised at another development; he did not seem to be afraid of them. However, not all the news was positive. He did seem withdrawn and was clearly sad.

As his strength continued to grow, the IPBC, the organization who works to place orphaned polar bears, began to study possible placements. The Alaska Zoo immediately came to mind but it was out of the question because they had no more room in their polar bear habitats.

The search for a placement widened. Sea World in San Diego, California began to show interest. One of the explorers in the rescue center had worked there and began to identify some positive reasons why the placement would be a good one. In fact, one of the medic team members expressed interest in traveling with the bear to the facility.

Arrangements were made and travel plans set. In February 2013, the yet unnamed orphan traveled to California to his new home.

It was not a good home for him. After his arrival he became listless and sad. He would not eat or play with the toys they gave him and his caretakers worried that he would starve.

The other polar bears already had friends and he really did not want to be with them anyway. He did not know what he wanted, but at night he dreamed of a beautiful brown-eyed girl. He had seen a lot of humans since he arrived at Sea World, but could only think of the one vision in his mind, a beautiful brown-eyed girl he saw looking at him through the glass.

The Sea World medical staff consulted experts in polar bear behavior all over the world. Something must be done.

One day shortly after Valentines Day, he looked up at a reflection he saw in the glass. Can it be true?

Those are the very eyes I see when I close my eyes. The beautiful eyes full of courage, hope and a new feeling for me of love. How can she find me? How will she know? What can I do?

He got up and went to the window. She was gone. He stayed in front of the window until sleep overtook him. She appeared again in his dream. Was he appearing in her dreams too? Where would she be next? How could he be happy?

He had never known any family. He did not know where he came from. He was totally alone. Suddenly a child was crying. The cub woke up to hear, "I want to go to the zoo!" What was a zoo? Would that make the child happy? Should he try to go there next?

His fate had already been decided.

The next day there was a meeting of his caregivers and a van came to transport him. He became afraid. He did not know where they were taking him The only word he understood was when somone said they were taking him to the zoo.

At the San Diego Zoo his enclosure seemed cooler and it was equipped with a beautiful pool. He was still alone, but he felt better, hopeful again.

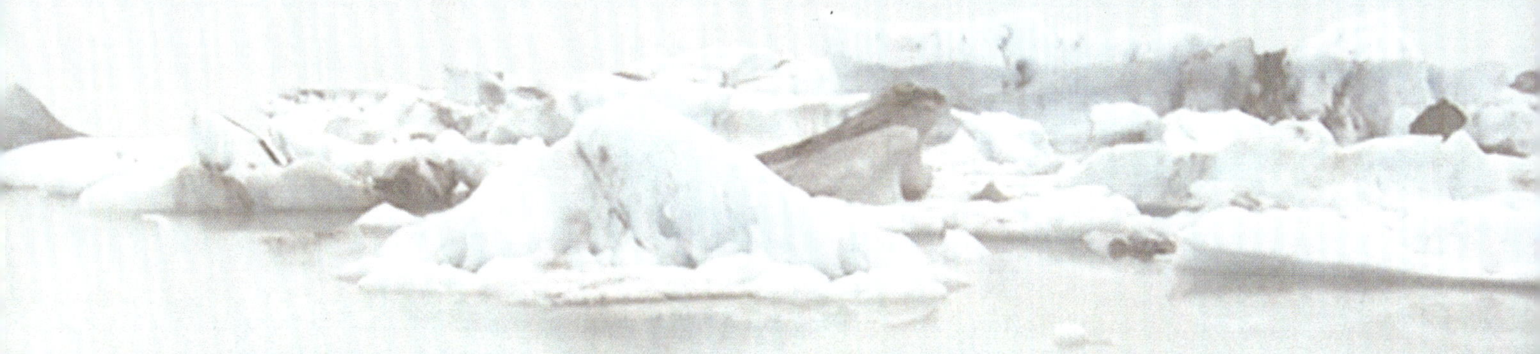

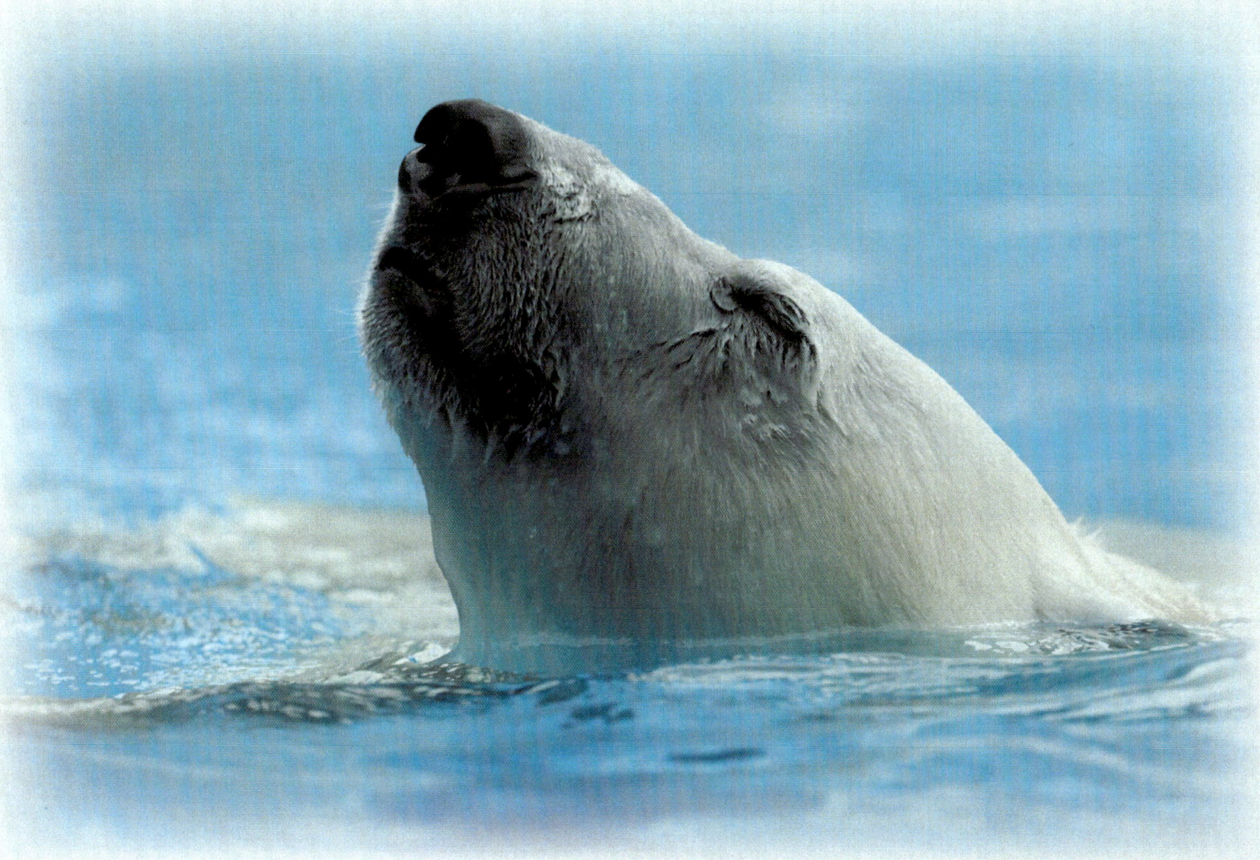

The next morning he woke up to see a group of children looking at him. What were they holding? Stuffed animals. Giraffes. Penguins. Hippos. Elephants. Pandas. Baby polar bears! The children were holding them closely, lovingly. Could this be the answer for him? Would the beautiful girl want him, hold him and love him if his spirit settled into a cuddly stuffed toy?

He closed his eyes and wished to be with the girl with the soft brown eyes. When he opened them the beautiful girl was there again. He closed his eyes even more tightly and wished with all his might that the two of them could be together.

Suddenly he felt himself being squeezed into a pile of dozens of other polar bears. They looked like him, with the exception of their eyes. The others had a fierce, menacing look in them. He didn't like that. The cub looked straight ahead.

Suddenly he was being lifted and he saw a woman who looked like the girl. Suddenly the woman was holding him out in front of her and telling the girl how beautiful his eyes were. They looked at the other stuffed polar bears piled around him and all of their eyes looked mean.

"Mom, I want this one. Look at his soft brown eyes. I think he loves me."

She took him from the store and outside into the sunlight. His dream had come true and so had hers.

Back in the cub's enclosure the cub picked up one of the many toys and tossed it up into the air. Then he ran into the pool as fast as his short legs would carry him and belly flopped into the water. The other cubs laughed, but he did not care. He had a connection they would never understand.

The beatiful girl sat with the soft, cuddly polar bear and looked lovingly at him. She said to him, " I will name you Awesome. We will be together forever!" That night the baby bear left the zoo with her. That night, as he went to sleep in her arms, he said, "It's Awesome."

And they lived happily ever after.

Edwards Brothers Malloy
Oxnard, CA USA
September 17, 2013